Hello, Family Members,

Learning to read is one of the most important accomplishments of early childhood. **Hello Reader!** books are designed to help children become skilled readers who like to read. Beginning readers learn to read by remembering frequently used words like "the," "is," and "and"; by using phonics skills to decode new words; and by interpreting picture and text clues. These books provide both the stories children enjoy and the structure they need to read fluently and independently. Here are suggestions for helping your child *before*, *during*, and *after* reading:

Before

- Look at the cover and pictures and have your child predict what the story is about.
- Read the story to your child.
- Encourage your child to chime in with familiar words and phrases.
- Echo read with your child by reading a line first and having your child read it after you do.

During

- Have your child think about a word he or she does not recognize right away. Provide hints such as "Let's see if we know the sounds" and "Have we read other words like this one?"
- Encourage your child to use phonics skills to sound out new words.
- Provide the word for your child when more assistance is needed so that he or she does not struggle and the experience of reading with you is a positive one.
- Encourage your child to have fun by reading with a lot of expression . . . like an actor!

After

- Have your child keep lists of interesting and favorite words.
- Encourage your child to read the books over and over again. Have him or her read to brothers, sisters, grandparents, and even teddy bears. Repeated readings develop confidence in young readers.
- Talk about the stories. Ask and answer questions. Share ideas about the funniest and most interesting characters and events in the stories.

I do hope that you and your child enjoy this book.

— Francie Alexander
 Chief Education Officer,
 Scholastic Education

To John-John and James Everett and Friends
—P.C.M. & R.L.M.

For my guys: Jimmy, Griffin, and Milo
—L.F.

Text copyright © 2003 by Patricia C. McKissack and Robert L. McKissack.
Illustrations copyright © 2003 by Laura Freeman.
All rights reserved. Published by Scholastic Inc.
SCHOLASTIC, HELLO READER, CARTWHEEL BOOKS, and associated logos
are trademarks and/or registered trademarks of Scholastic Inc.

Library of Congress Cataloging-in-Publication Data

McKissack, Patricia, 1944-
  Itching and twitching / by Patricia C. McKissack and Robert L. McKissack ;
illustrated by Laura Freeman.
    p. cm.— (Hello Reader! Level 4)
  Summary: Monkey, who scratches when he itches, and Rabbit, who twitches when
he feels like it, try to accept each other and themselves.
    ISBN 0-439-24224-X (alk. paper)
    [1. Folklore—Nigeria.] I. McKissack, Robert L. II. Freeman, Laura, ill.
III. Title. IV. Series.
    PZ8.1.M199 It 2003
    398.2'09669'0452932—dc21
                             2001032229

10 9 8 7 6 5 4 3 2 1   03 04 05 06 07

Printed in the U.S.A. 24 • First printing, February 2003

Itching and Twitching

A Nigerian Folktale

Adapted by Patricia C. McKissack
and Robert L. McKissack

Illustrated by Laura Freeman

Hello Reader! — Level 4

SCHOLASTIC INC.
Cartwheel
·B·O·O·K·S· ®

New York   Toronto   London   Auckland   Sydney
Mexico City   New Delhi   Hong Kong   Buenos Aires

Rabbit and Monkey were neighbors.
One day they met at the water hole.
"I am cooking a big pot of stew," said Monkey.
"Please come have dinner with me tonight."

Rabbit was excited.
"I will be there," he answered.

Monkey gathered vegetables from
his garden.
He put a big pot on the stove.
He filled the pot with meat, potatoes,
carrots, onions, and a little bit of
okra for flavor.

At sunset—not a minute early
or a minute late—Rabbit arrived
at Monkey's house.

"Everything is ready," said Monkey.

All during the meal,
Monkey itched.
He took a bite of stew.
Then he scratched his leg,

his arm,

his head,

behind his left ear,

and even between his toes.

Rabbit was no better.
He could not stop twitching.
Rabbit took a bite of stew.
Then his ears twitched—
so did his nose and his feet.
He kept moving all the time.

When the meal was over,
they went outside to sit under the stars.

Rabbit could not be still.
And Monkey could not stop scratching.

Rabbit's twitching got so bad that
Monkey had to say something.
"What kind of a guest are you?"
he shouted.
"Can't you be still for one minute?
Your twitching bothers me!"

"Me?" Rabbit shouted. "Look at you!
You are the one who is scratching
and scratching and scratching!
At least I can be still if I choose!"

"You can't stop twitching for
one minute!" said Monkey.
"But I can stop scratching, for sure."

"No, you can't," said Rabbit, laughing.

"Let's put it to a test," said Monkey.
"The first one to scratch or twitch
must do all the dishes."

Rabbit agreed.

Monkey sat on his stool.
He folded his arms.
He was itching everywhere.
He wanted to scratch,
but he did not even move a toe.

Rabbit sat across from him.
He was as still as a stone.
He wanted to move,
but he would not.

The itching was so awful,
Monkey had to think of a way
to scratch himself.
But he did not want to lose the bet.
Suddenly, he got an idea.
He hopped to his feet.
"I want to tell you a story."

Rabbit liked stories.
"Okay," he said.
Anything to take his mind off
wanting to twitch.

Monkey began his story.
"One day, a king went hunting.
He came upon a magic plum tree.
It was being eaten away by ants.
The king felt sorry for the tree.
He stopped and took care of the tree,
saving it from the ants.

"Thankful for his help, the tree dropped
golden plums to reward the king.
One plum fell on the king's arm.
Then one fell on his head,
then on his leg . . . ."

Monkey touched his arm,
his head, and his leg. . . .
He touched every body
part he named from
head to toe.

Rabbit did not move—
not even the tip of his ear.

When Monkey finished his story,
Rabbit said, "Now, I will tell *you* a story."
He began.
"Once there was a king,
who had three sons and one daughter.
He sent them to rule over all his lands.
One prince went to the North."
Here Rabbit turned his head in that direction.

"Another prince went to the East."
Rabbit pointed his ear in that direction.

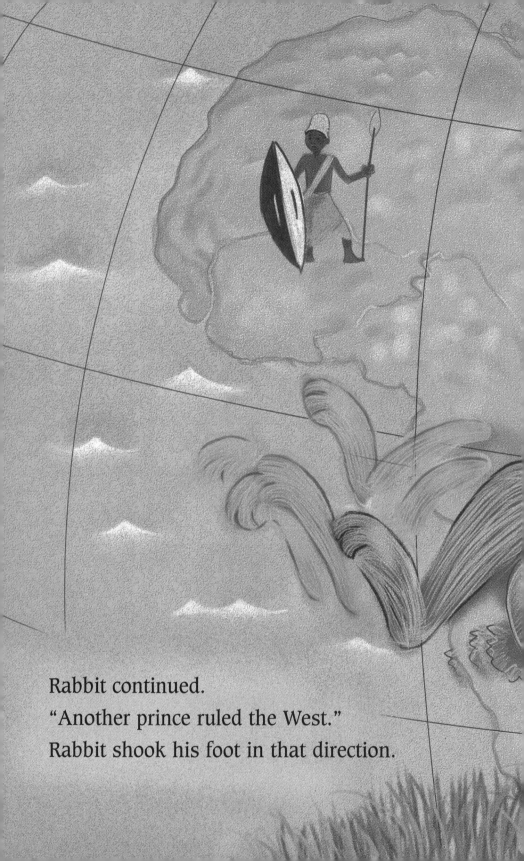

Rabbit continued.
"Another prince ruled the West."
Rabbit shook his foot in that direction.

"And the beautiful princess ruled the South."
Rabbit leaned his whole body in that direction.

"Stop! Rabbit, stop!" shouted Monkey.
"You can't fool me!
You are twitching as you tell your story.
So, you lose the bet!"

Rabbit leaped high into the air.
"I did no worse than you!
You did not fool me.
You were scratching
when you told your story!"

Monkey shrugged.
"I can't help it!
I am a monkey.
Monkeys scratch where they itch!"

Rabbit nodded.
"I understand," he said.
"I am a rabbit, and rabbits twitch.
We are just being ourselves—
a monkey and a rabbit.
Neither one of us should lose the bet
for being who we are."

"Let's agree that as friends,
we will enjoy each other
just the way we are," said Monkey.

"Agreed," said Rabbit.

Later, Rabbit and Monkey
did the dishes—together.
Monkey put away the last dinner plate.
Rabbit hung up the dishcloth.

Then they spent the rest of the evening
telling stories—
and itching and twitching.